Houdini's Escape

Susan Hughes

Illustrated by
Leanne Franson

Scholastic Canada Ltd.
Toronto New York London Auckland Sydney
Mexico City New Delhi Hong Kong Buenos Aires

Scholastic Canada Ltd.
604 King Street West, Toronto, Ontario M5V 1E1, Canada

Scholastic Inc.
557 Broadway, New York, NY 10012, USA

Scholastic Australia Pty Limited
PO Box 579, Gosford, NSW 2250, Australia

Scholastic New Zealand Limited
Private Bag 94407, Botany, Manukau 2163, New Zealand

Scholastic Children's Books
Euston House, 24 Eversholt Street, London NW1 1DB, UK

www.scholastic.ca

Library and Archives Canada Cataloguing in Publication
Hughes, Susan, 1960-, author
Houdini's escape / Susan Hughes ; illustrated by Leanne Franson.
(The puppy collection ; 7)
Issued in print and electronic formats.
ISBN 978-1-4431-4650-0 (paperback).--ISBN 978-1-4431-4803-0 (html).--
ISBN 978-1-4431-4804-7 (Apple)
I. Franson, Leanne, illustrator II. Title. III. Series: Hughes, Susan, 1960-
Puppy collection ; 7.
PS8565.U42H68 2016 jC813'.54 C2015-905113-4
C2015-905114-2

Thank you to Dr. Stephanie Avery, DVM, for her puppy expertise.

Cover Credits:
Cover: Beagle© AnetaPics/Shutterstock.com.
Logo: © Mat Hayward/Shutterstock.com; © Michael Pettigrew/Shutterstock.com; © Picture-Pets/Shutterstock.com. Background: © Anne Precious/Shutterstock.com; © dip/Shutterstock.com. Back cover: pendant © Little Wale/Shutterstock.com.

6 5 4 3 2 1 Printed in Canada 121 16 17 18 19 20

MIX
Paper from
responsible sources
FSC® C004071

For my dear friend Jan Kosick and her sweet little puppies Coco and Murphy

CHAPTER ONE

Kat was watching a parade of puppies. They were so sweet! Each puppy was prancing along. Each one was wagging its tail. Each one was looking at her hopefully.

There was a poodle and a Labrador retriever. There was a Dalmatian and a bulldog. There was a German shepherd and a whippet. The parade of puppies went on and on!

It was Thursday afternoon. Kat was having her

favourite daydream. She was leaning against a tree in the park. Her eyes were closed.

The parade was over. Now all the puppies played and tumbled together in front of Kat.

A Pomeranian with tiny paws ran in circles around a basset hound puppy with droopy ears. A West Highland terrier and a boxer pup chased each other across the lawn and back. An Airedale puppy chased its tail around and around.

"Make up your mind, Katherine," her mother said.

"Yes," said her father. "Which puppy would you like for your very own?"

"Kat?" a voice called.

Which puppy would I like? The sweet Shih Tzu with the black button nose? The adorable German shepherd pup rolling in the grass? The playful Newfoundland with the wobbly tummy?

"Kat-nip?" It was Maya. "Yoo-hoo, Kat!"

Kat's daydream ended. She opened her eyes.

Kat loved dogs more than anything in the whole wide world. But her parents weren't *really* letting her choose a puppy of her own. Her parents said they didn't have enough time to look after one.

Kat almost didn't mind now, because her aunt had opened Tails Up! Grooming and Boarding in their town of Orchard Valley. Aunt Jenn groomed the dogs, and her receptionist, Tony, answered the phone and booked appointments. The salon was very busy. In fact, it was so successful that Aunt Jenn often needed help when puppies came to board. Aunt Jenn knew how much Kat and her friends loved puppies, so she counted on them to lend a hand.

"Kat, come on!" Maya called from the doorway of Grace's house. Kat, Maya and Grace had come there straight from school.

Grace is so lucky, Kat thought, as she crossed the street to join Maya. *Her house is right across from the park.* Kat loved the park in any season.

It was the best place to bring puppies to play!

"Why did you want to wait out here for us? Weren't you cold?" Maya asked. Shivering, she shoved her hands into her pockets. "Let me guess. You wanted some time for a little daydreaming, right, Kat-nip?"

Kat grinned and rolled her eyes. Maya knew her so well! She knew that Kat daydreamed about getting her own puppy. Maya also thought it was hilarious that a girl who loved dogs so much would be called Kat, short for Katherine. That's why Maya nicknamed her Kat-nip.

Kat didn't mind. Maya only teased her in fun. Plus, Kat was used to it. Maya had been doing it almost as long as she and Kat could talk. That's how long the girls had been friends. They didn't even remember a time when they didn't know each other. They lived on opposite sides of Orchard Valley, but they had gone to the same nursery school. They had played soccer together. They had been in the same class at school until this year.

They liked many of the same things, especially dogs. Now they both liked the new girl at school, Grace, too!

"Okay! All set!" Grace called. She hurried out of her house, closing the door behind her.

Grace had moved to Orchard Valley that autumn and was in Kat's grade four-five class. It took some time for Kat and Maya to get to know Grace. But they found out that she was kind and a bit shy. Like them, she loved dogs.

"So what did your mom say, Grace? And what about your parents, Maya?" asked Kat. "Can you two come to Tails Up?"

Aunt Jenn had called Kat at her house at lunchtime. Maya was there too, as usual. They liked to take turns eating lunch at each other's house. Aunt Jenn had asked if Kat and her friends could come to Tails Up after school. She wanted to speak to the girls about a new puppy boarder.

Kat's mom had said Kat could go, but Maya hadn't had time to call her mother and ask — it was time to hurry back to school.

That's why the three girls headed to Grace's house when school ended for the day. Grace needed to ask her mom if she could go to Tails Up, and Maya needed to phone her parents, too.

"Mom said I can come!" Grace said, grinning.

"Maya?" asked Kat. "You can come, too?"

"*Exactamente*!" Maya said.

Kat, Maya and Grace did a high-five.

"Come on, tremendous trio. Let's make like a banana and split!" said Maya.

The girls headed out toward Tails Up. But they hadn't gone far before Grace cried, "Hey! The joke of the day! We got distracted after school. Kat, you never told us the answer."

Every morning Kat told a joke. She always made the girls wait before she told them the answer.

"Oh my!" Maya moaned dramatically. "Grace, I don't think I can bear to hear the answer. Can you?"

"Good point," said Grace.

"Very funny." Kat grinned. "The joke was, How did the little Scottish dog feel when it saw a monster?"

Maya and Grace pretended they couldn't hear anything.

Kat laughed. "You know you want the answer. You know you do!" she teased.

Maya shrugged. "All right. If you insist, Kat-nip."

"Okay. Here goes: The little Scottish dog felt . . . terrier-fied," said Kat. "Get it? Terrified? Terrier-fied?"

"Oh, so bad! That actually hurt." Maya rubbed her ears.

"So, so bad!" Grace agreed. She rolled her eyes.

"Why, thank you," said Kat, with a bow and a giggle.

Laughing, the three girls grabbed at one another's arms and began to run toward Tails Up together.

CHAPTER TWO

The bell on the front door jingled as the girls entered the grooming salon, Tony was on the phone. He waved to the girls from behind the front desk.

Grace headed straight for Tony's cat, Marmalade. The elderly tabby cat insisted on going everywhere with Tony. She adored him but ignored everyone else. While she was at Tails Up, she didn't move from the counter.

From there, she looked down on all the dogs.

Marmalade didn't look at Grace as Grace stroked the cat's back. But within seconds, Grace heard the tabby's loud purring.

"Just a moment, please," Tony said politely into the phone. He covered the receiver with his hand.

"Ladies! Hello!" he said to the girls. He looked at his watch. He pointed at the grooming room and then held up two fingers. "Jenn will be out in two minutes." Tony leaned forward and whispered, "If she's not, the clients will begin to grumble . . . and growl!"

Kat laughed and gave him a thumbs-up.

"Okay, quick," Maya said to Kat. "Pick a person. We only have two minutes."

Kat and Maya liked to play a game. They liked to choose a person and guess the dog breed he or she most resembled. If the person had a dog, they liked to see if the person and the dog matched.

Kat looked around the waiting room. There was a small couch and three chairs. There was a scale and shelves lined with dog food. Two women sat together on the couch. They were each reading a section of the same newspaper. A Great Dane lay across both their feet. His head extended beyond one end of the couch. His tail stretched out beyond the other end.

A young man sat in one of the chairs. He was texting on his phone. Kat saw he was holding a leash, but where was his dog? She followed the leash with her eyes. It led behind the couch. Kat shifted to one side and peeked behind the couch. A golden doodle had squeezed itself between the couch and the wall. The dog's sad eyes said to Kat,"Don't tell anyone where I am and maybe I won't have to be clipped!"

An older man sat in another chair. He had short curly hair and a long curly beard, both a golden colour. He wore a tan-coloured leather

coat with fringe. His boots were fringed, too.

Maya gestured toward the man. "Your aunt must be grooming his dog. What do you think?"

Kat studied the man for a moment. "Wheaten terrier. For sure."

Maya nodded. "Agreed."

Just then, the door to the grooming studio opened. A dog came bounding out. He was covered in curly fur that was the colour of yellow wheat — from his ears to his tummy to his tail.

"Yes!" Maya whispered to Kat. "A wheatie! We guessed it!"

Aunt Jenn appeared holding the end of the leash. She wore her pink grooming coat. Her brown hair was pulled back in a ponytail.

"Here's Prince for you, Mr. Renzo," said Aunt Jenn.

The man with the curly hair jumped up. "Oh, you've done a wonderful job!" Mr. Renzo said. He bent down to greet his dog. "Prince looks as handsome as a . . . prince!"

"Thank you," Aunt Jenn said. "But grooming him was a challenge, Mr. Renzo. Lots of hair! Too much hair!" She gave Prince a quick pat on the head. She handed Mr. Renzo the leash. "I know you want your wheaten terrier to look good. This means Prince needs his hair cut more often."

Mr. Renzo blushed. He tugged at the curled ends of his beard.

"His coat was quite shaggy. And it was touching the floor, Mr. Renzo," said Aunt Jenn gently.

"Yes, you're quite right," Mr. Renzo agreed. He stroked Prince's head. "I'll come more often. I will. Thank you again."

Mr. Renzo went to the counter to pay his bill.

Aunt Jenn turned to the girls. "Hello, my Kitty-Kat!" she said. This was her special name for Kat. "And hello, Maya and Grace."

The girls smiled.

"We can't wait to meet the new puppy, Aunt Jenn," Kat said.

Aunt Jenn turned to the clients who were waiting. "I'll just be a moment," she told them. "My puppy helpers and I have special puppy business to attend to!"

With a toss of her ponytail, Aunt Jenn briskly led the girls to the doggy-daycare room. She was about to open the door but then paused. Her eyes twinkled. "When we go in, be very quiet," she said.

She opened the door. She and the girls quietly stepped into the room. Then Aunt Jenn signalled them to stop. She tapped her ear to tell them to listen.

Kat listened closely. All of a sudden she could hear it — a gentle snoring sound. She giggled. Quickly she scanned the room. The doggy-daycare room was large. It had shelves and a fenced-in area, like a playpen. There was a back door that led to a large yard. A stairway led up to a big room where Aunt Jenn could do dog training. Her apartment was also upstairs.

Most importantly, it had four dog kennels in a row under the window along one wall. Although today Kat saw that there were five dog kennels there. There were four regular kennels and a new blue one. The snoring sound was coming from the blue kennel.

Inside the kennel, a puppy was curled up, lying in the sunshine.

"Presenting . . . Houdini!" Aunt Jenn announced.

The little puppy woke up as Kat, Grace and Maya hurried over to greet him. Houdini jumped to his feet. He gave a big yawn. He put his hind end in the air and gave a little wiggle stretch.

Kat giggled. *The puppy looks so soft and cuddly*, she thought. *I can't wait to pick him up and hug him!*

"Oh, he's so sweet!" cooed Grace.

"He certainly is!" agreed Aunt Jenn. "Houdini is a three-month-old beagle. He's very friendly and full of energy. He has been with his owner, Gordon Ho, for four weeks."

Houdini's head, ears and part of his face were tan. He had faint tan spots on his front legs. His back was black and so was the top half of his tail. He had a white stripe down his face, and his muzzle was white. So was his chest, his belly and most of his back legs. The end of his tail was white, too.

"You're adorable, little Houdini!" said Maya.

The puppy wagged his tail. He smiled at the girls.

"Houdini knows two commands: *sit* and *down*. Gordon hasn't taught Houdini to come yet," explained Aunt Jenn. "That's next."

"We can help Houdini practise *sit* and *down,*" said Kat.

"Just like you did with Riley and Piper," said Aunt Jenn. "That would be good."

Riley and Piper were puppies that had boarded at Tails Up. Riley was a three-month-old golden retriever puppy, and Piper was a sweet four-month-old Bernese mountain dog. The girls had helped both the puppies practise their commands. And now they would get to practise with Houdini as well!

"Today is Thursday," said Aunt Jenn. "Mr. Ho is only out of town until Sunday." She popped a piece of gum in her mouth. "I can look after Houdini in the evenings. Could you girls play with Houdini now and tomorrow after school? And take him for a walk on Saturday?"

"I can," said Kat.

"Me too," said Maya.

"I can't help Saturday," said Grace. "My family is spending the afternoon with my granny. But I can help today and tomorrow!"

"Excellent," said Aunt Jenn. She did a little cha-cha-cha dance.

Then she pointed to an area on the floor that was covered with newspapers. "We are helping to house-train Houdini. Please put him on the newspapers every once in a while, or when he is peeing or you think he is about to pee. That way he'll learn that he can't go wherever he wants and that there is a proper place to pee. At first he'll pee inside on the newspaper and then he'll learn to wait until he can go outside."

Aunt Jenn popped her gum. "Here is Houdini's leash," she said. "And these are the dog biscuits he likes. You can use them as rewards when he uses the newspaper or obeys your commands.

Any questions?"

"This blue crate doesn't look like the Tails Up crates," Grace said.

"You're right," said Aunt Jenn. "It's Houdini's crate."

"Houdini has his own crate? Why?" asked Maya. "I thought crates were only used in doggy-daycare centres!"

"Many people use a crate with their puppies," said Aunt Jenn. "Puppies enjoy curling up in a crate. It feels like a den to them — nice and cozy."

"Our dog Bella had a crate when she was a puppy," said Grace. Before Grace moved to Orchard Valley, she lived on a farm. Her collie Bella died just before Grace and her family moved to town. "Bella liked to sleep in it. It made her feel safe when she was little. Also, it helped us to house-train her."

"That's right," said Aunt Jenn. "Most puppies

will not dirty the place where they sleep. When they're in the crate, they control themselves. They learn where it's okay to pee and not to pee."

"Plus many puppies get into mischief whenever they can!" said Grace. "When we were out and Bella was alone, we always put her in her crate. Mom and Dad didn't want her to chew our furniture or rugs!"

Maya crouched by Houdini. "So, we can tell from your snoring that you seem to be happy in your crate, Houdini," she said. "But would you like to come out and play?"

The puppy wagged his tail. The girls laughed.

"I think that's a big 'yes'!" said Aunt Jenn. "Have fun with Houdini, girls. Now hi-ho, hi-ho, it's back to work I go!"

Aunt Jenn gave a little wave and off she went.

CHAPTER THREE

"It's hard to get the door on Houdini's crate open," Grace said. "The clasp is tricky to open."

Grace started to laugh. The beagle puppy was pressing his nose against the door while Grace worked on the latch. Then Houdini began licking Grace's fingers through the bars. "Hey, Houdini! That tickles!" Grace said, and she scooted away from the crate.

"We may have to get your aunt to help us open

that latch," Grace said to Kat. "It's completely stuck."

"Grace, do you want me to try?" Maya asked. "Maybe . . ."

Just then, the door popped open, and Houdini came tumbling out! The puppy quickly scrambled to his feet. He stood proudly in front of them, wagging his tail.

"Hey! How did you do that?" asked Kat.

Houdini bounded over to Kat and put his front paws up on her knees. He wagged his tail even more.

"How did that happen?" said Grace, puzzled. "I couldn't budge that latch!"

"It's magic! Magic!" announced Maya. She twirled in a circle with her arms held wide, pretending to wave a wand.

Kat giggled and picked up Houdini. "How did you escape from there, little guy? Is that why you're named Houdini?"

"Houdini . . ." said Grace thoughtfully. "Wasn't he a famous magician?"

"Yes — and an escape artist, too," Maya said. "I did a project on Harry Houdini last year. Houdini was strapped into a straitjacket. Then he was dangled upside down from a crane. He escaped while everyone watched!"

"That's amazing," said Grace.

"And so are you," Kat told Houdini. She stroked

the puppy's ears. They were as soft as silk!

"Harry Houdini also escaped from jails, handcuffs, ropes and chains," Maya said. She tapped Houdini on the head with her pretend wand. "But you're not going to try to escape from anywhere else, are you, little puppy?"

Houdini yipped. His eyes sparkled. He wagged his tail energetically.

"I'm not sure he's agreeing!" Kat giggled, setting the puppy down on the floor. "We'll have to keep an eye on him. But for now, it's time to play!"

"Here you go, Houdini," called Grace. She picked up a chew toy from a basket of dog toys and waved it. "Come and get it!"

Houdini's ears perked up, and he ran to Grace.

"Ready, puppy? Go get it!" Grace threw the toy across the room. Houdini tumbled after it. He pounced on the toy and shook it in his mouth.

"Bring it back, now, Houdini," called Maya. "Bring it here!"

The puppy ignored Maya. He growled and chewed on the toy. When it squeaked, Houdini's eyes opened wide. He dropped the toy in surprise. The girls laughed.

Suddenly Houdini spread his legs and squatted.

"Oopsie!" cried Kat. "Remember what we were saying about house-training? Hang on there, little guy!"

Quickly she ran over and scooped up the puppy. She set him on the newspapers, which were laid out on the floor nearby.

"Just in time!" Kat said, as Houdini peed on the newspaper.

"Good one, Houdini," said Grace. "You'll be house-trained in no time."

The girls decided to play ball with Houdini. Maya threw a red plastic ball across the room for the puppy, and Houdini chased it. When he wouldn't give it up, they decided to use a trick they had learned from playing with some of the other Tails Up boarding puppies.

Kat picked up a blue ball from the basket.

"Look, Houdini!" Kat said. "A nice blue ball for you!"

Houdini looked at Kat, the red ball firmly in his mouth.

Kat threw the blue ball across the room. Instantly, Houdini dropped the red ball. He raced across the room after the blue ball, his floppy brown ears flying. When he reached the ball, the beagle puppy tried to stop, but he was going too fast. Houdini slid across the room, the blue ball caught between his legs. Finally he came to a gentle stop just as he reached the wall.

"Oh, Houdini!" Grace giggled. "Are you okay?"

The puppy jumped up and grabbed the red ball in his mouth. He wagged his tail, waiting for more fun.

"Okay then!" Grace tossed the red ball across the room, and Houdini scooted after it.

The girls took turns throwing balls for Houdini, over and over again. Three times, he flopped down and rested. Three times, the energetic beagle puppy bounded back onto his feet. He wanted to play again.

Finally, Kat said, "Now that Houdini has had some play time, let's practise some commands with him."

The girls practised *sit* and *lie down* with Houdini. They used hand signals and word commands. They gave him a treat every time he did what he was told.

When it was time for the girls to leave, Kat could hardly bear to say goodbye. She picked up the puppy and pulled him close. She breathed in the wonderful puppy smell.

"Goodbye, Houdini," she said, as she placed him back in his crate. "See you tomorrow afternoon."

CHAPTER FOUR

The bell rang. School was over for the week. Kat and Grace quickly put their books in their backpacks, jumped up and hurried across the room.

"You both have that look on your face," said their teacher, Ms. Mitchell. "That look of puppy love! Are you off to Tails Up?"

Kat and Grace grinned. Ms. Mitchell knew how much the two girls loved dogs. She knew they often helped out at Aunt Jenn's grooming studio when there were puppies boarding.

"Yes, we are, Ms. Mitchell," said Kat.

"There's a little beagle puppy waiting there for us," explained Grace happily. "And then Maya and Kat are coming to my place for dinner for the first time."

"Oh, what fun! Have a good time with the puppy — and with one another," said Ms. Mitchell. "And enjoy the rest of the weekend, girls!"

"You too," said Kat.

Kat and Grace ran across the schoolyard. Maya waved to them from the gate. "Let's go, slow pokes," she cried.

The three friends chatted cheerfully all the way to Tails Up.

When they arrived at the grooming salon, there were several clients with their dogs in the waiting room. The girls waved hello to Tony and were about to hurry past when Tony called out, "Ladies!"

The girls came over to the counter. "What's up, Tony?" Maya asked.

"Jenn is busy grooming a lively cocker spaniel right now. But the bestest boss ever wanted me to give you a message about Houdini." As Tony spoke, Marmalade glared at the girls. She rosc, stalked along the counter and lay down directly in front of the girls, with her back to them.

The girls laughed.

"I think Marmalade is trying to give you a message, too!" Tony said, with a grin.

"We understand. You need some attention, don't you?" Maya murmured sympathetically. She stroked the elderly cat. Marmalade immediately began to purr.

"So," Tony said, "the beagle puppy's name — Houdini? Well, Mr. Ho, the puppy's owner, named the puppy after the real Houdini. He said the puppy is a bit of an escape artist himself. So your aunt says to take special care with the little fellow."

The girls grinned at one another. They had already guessed that!

"The boss says to play in the backyard with Houdini today and leave the park for tomorrow," said Tony. "Just in case."

"Good idea!" said Kat. The Tails Up backyard was a nice place to play with puppies. It was enclosed by a chain-link fence. It had a lawn and flower beds. There were bushes and trees along one side. There was a smaller fenced-in area along the other side. A back gate led out to a laneway, which opened onto the side street. It was a good shortcut to the park.

The girls headed for the doggy-daycare room. But before they went in, Kat stopped them. "Wait!" She put a finger across her lips. "Let's creep in without waking Houdini. Maybe we can hear him snoring again, like yesterday!"

Grace giggled. "Before yesterday I never knew that dogs snore."

"Well, most dogs don't. It's mostly brachycephalic dogs that snore," said Kat.

"Bracky what?" said Grace.

"Brachycephalic," repeated Kat. She tried to keep her voice low. "They are dogs with short noses and flat faces. You know, like pugs or bulldogs. Often the top part of their airway is blocked. They might have narrow nostrils. Or it can be blocked by that soft tissue that hangs down from the roofs of their mouths."

"Soft tissue?" repeated Grace.

"Yes," said Kat. "Dogs need that soft tissue when they eat. It blocks off their airways when they swallow, to keep water or food from going into their lungs by mistake."

Now Maya and Grace grinned. They didn't say anything.

"But in brachycephalic dogs, the tissue is especially long. It hangs down farther. And this flattens their windpipes and makes them have trouble breathing. When they sleep, they snore," Kat explained. "Sometimes they even snort when they're awake!"

Maya and Grace were still grinning.

"What?" Kat said.

"Nothing, oh, Einstein of the dog world!" said Maya. She made googly eyes at Kat. "We're only

thinking that you know more about dogs than anyone else in the whole wide world. Right, Grace?"

"Right," agreed Grace.

Kat laughed. Her friends knew that her favourite book was *Dog Breeds of the World*. She had read it over one hundred times. She also spent hours reading about dogs on thc Internet. She loved learning everything she could about dogs.

But now Grace was looking puzzled. "But, Kat, Houdini doesn't have a flat face. Houdini isn't a pug or a bulldog — he's a beagle!" said Grace. "So why does *he* snore?"

"Because many beagles have extra-long soft tissuey stuff, too." Kat smiled. "That is, according to—"

"*Dog Breeds of the World*," chanted all three girls. They couldn't help it. They burst into loud laughter.

"I think Houdini probably heard that," giggled Maya.

Sure enough, when they opened the door, the puppy was standing in his crate with his ears perked. He wagged his white-tipped tail in excitement.

"Houdini, hello!" cooed Kat. "How are you?"

The girls dropped their backpacks and jackets and hurried over.

"You haven't escaped from your crate today. Good puppy!" said Maya.

Houdini wagged his tail even faster. He pushed at his crate door with his nose.

"Oh, are you going to open it yourself again?" Grace chuckled. "The latch probably won't be as stiff this time, and I can actually do it for you!"

Grace was right. She unlatched the door easily, and the beagle puppy came barrelling out immediately. He collided with Grace's legs. Then he tried to jump up on Grace, wiggling

happily. But when Grace bent down to pick him up, the puppy scooted over to Kat.

Houdini squirmed against Kat's legs. When Kat bent down to plant a kiss on Houdini's head, he galloped over to greet Maya.

Maya only had time to pet the puppy once before he was off again. He trotted straight to the newspaper, squatted and peed.

"Good boy!" the girls cheered.

Off again, the puppy headed for the basket

of dog toys. He took the closest toy, which was a plastic bone. He shook it in his mouth and growled. Then he dropped the toy and continued exploring.

Houdini sniffed around the shelves. He sniffed the big bag of dog food. He sniffed the girls' backpacks and Kat's and Grace's jackets. Then Houdini pounced on Maya's jacket and began dragging it across the floor.

"Hey, you!" Maya said, as she rescued her jacket from Houdini. "This puppy has so much energy! Let's take him outside right away."

"Good idea," said Kat. "Let's go."

The girls put on their jackets. Kat grabbed Houdini's leash, which was hanging from the wall near his basket. "Just in case," she said.

Grace gathered up a few dog toys, and Maya took a handful of dog treats.

"Okay. Come on, Houdini," Kat called, opening the door to the backyard. "Let's go outside!"

Houdini's ears perked up. He lifted his little black nose and smelled the air. Then he scooted across the room and out the door.

"Look at him go!" said Maya. She smiled as she, Grace and Kat ran out after him.

Then suddenly Grace cried, "Oh no!"

Kat froze. The puppy was halfway across the yard, and the back gate, which led to the laneway, was wide open.

The puppy was making a beeline for the gate.

CHAPTER FIVE

"Houdini!" Kat called. "Come back, Houdini!

The puppy didn't know the command come. He didn't look back. He didn't slow down.

Kat began to run after the puppy. "Houdini! Come back!"

"Houdini! Come, Houdini!" called Maya and Grace.

The puppy kept going. He slipped out the gate and — *poof!* — he was gone.

Kat's heart sank, but she ran even faster. She had to catch him. She had to. If he went down the laneway toward the road . . .

Don't think. Just run! Kat ordered herself.

Kat reached the back gate and raced through it into the laneway. She looked to the right. That way the laneway ran behind other backyards and stopped at a dead end. No Houdini.

She looked the other way. There was Houdini, bounding toward the street, his ears flapping.

"Houdini!" Kat cried, trying to make her voice sound enticing. "Oh, Houdini, look what I have! Come here, Houdini. I have a treat for you!"

The puppy didn't slow down.

Kat began sprinting toward him. *I can't possibly catch him before he gets to the street. What if he goes out onto the road? What if a car is coming?*

"Houdini, come here! Come here!" Kat called, desperately.

All of a sudden, a little girl was there on the sidewalk, at the end of the laneway. To Kat, she looked about seven years old, and she was all alone.

"Please! Stop that puppy!" Kat called to the girl. "Please!"

But the little girl had already seen the puppy. She had turned down the laneway and walked toward Houdini with her hand out. She was calling softly to him.

Now she was bending down, smiling. The beagle puppy ran right up to her. He sniffed her hand and wiggled happily. He wagged his tail.

Kat heard the girl say, "Hello there, puppy. Just where do you think you're going?"

She saw the little girl hook her fingers under Houdini's collar.

Kat came to a stop in front of the girl, breathing heavily. Maya and Grace were right behind her.

“Thank you!” Kat said to the girl. “Thank you so much!”

“Can I pick up the puppy?” the girl asked. “He looks so sweet!”

“Kiera!” called a woman. She had just come running around the corner, into the laneway. “Kiera! You vanished again! I thought I’d lost you!” She hurried over. “What’s happening? Is everything all right?”

“Oh yes,” said Kat. “Your little girl — Kiera — just helped us!”

“We’re looking after this puppy,” explained Maya. “He sneaked out the back gate into the laneway, and Kiera caught him for us.”

The woman nodded. “Kiera loves puppies.” She smiled. “I’m Kiera’s mother, Janet. We were just heading to the park. I stopped for a moment to get something out of my backpack — and Kiera was gone! She has a habit of wandering away on her own." Kiera's mother looked down at the girl, who was still cuddling Houdini. "I have to keep a close eye on you, don't I, Kiera?"

Kiera looked up and smiled happily. "Yes," she agreed. She turned to Kat. "What's your puppy's name? He's so sweet!"

Kat explained that Houdini was boarding at Tails Up and that she, Maya and Grace were looking after him until Sunday.

"Thank you so much for catching our escape artist puppy," repeated Grace.

"I wish there was something we could do to thank you," Kat said.

"I know!" Kiera's eyes lit up. "My cousin Charles is having a birthday party for his dog. I'm going, but I don't have a dog to bring. Could I bring Houdini? Please? It would be so much fun!"

"The party is tomorrow afternoon at a play park for pets," Kiera's mother explained. "I'm sure my sister, Brenda, would love it if the three of you could bring Houdini to the party."

Kiera's mother told the girls all the details about the party. Then Kiera added, "Mom can't come to the party tomorrow. She has to work. But my babysitter is taking me. She's really nice and she loves dogs, too." Kiera patted Houdini. "I know she would love to meet Houdini."

"We'll have to check with Aunt Jenn and our parents, but we'll bring Houdini if we can," Kat promised. "And thank you again for catching this little rascal."

"You're welcome," said Kiera. She gave Houdini a kiss on the head. "Bye, puppy! I hope I see you tomorrow!"

CHAPTER SIX

"You won't give us the slip again, you naughty puppy!" scolded Kat. "I'm making sure the gate is closed properly this time!"

Houdini didn't seem to mind. When Kat set him down inside the Tails Up yard, he bounded cheerfully about, his ears flying out to the sides.

"Houdini looks like he might just lift off," said Grace, giggling.

Maya ran into the doggy-daycare room. In a

moment she was back, snapping photos of the puppy.

Houdini pounced on a branch in the garden. He grabbed it in his mouth and dragged it across the yard. Then he sniffed a pile of leaves. He suddenly began burrowing into them. Soon all the girls could see was his white-tipped tail wagging through the leaves.

"He is so cute," giggled Kat.

Grace grabbed a stick from the garden. "Here, Houdini," she called. "Let's play tug-of-war!" She shook the stick. Houdini ran over and grabbed the end in his mouth. Grace pulled the stick, and Houdini tugged.

When the puppy stopped for a rest, the girls agreed that it was a good time to practise his commands. Kat clipped Houdini's leash to his collar. Maya pulled out the dog treats. She went first, using hand gestures and words. She asked him to sit and then lie down. When

Houdini did what he was told, Maya gave him a treat. Then Grace had a turn.

"Good boy," she told him, when he obeyed her commands.

"Now we'll practise *come.* That's the one you need the most practice with," Kat said. She held Houdini's leash and stood a few steps away from the puppy.

Maya crouched by Houdini and held him in place.

Kat made some interesting noises. She showed Houdini the treat. She danced around a bit to make sure she had the puppy's attention. That was very important. Then she said, "Houdini. Come."

Maya let go of Houdini, and he leaped forward and bounded toward Kat.

"Good puppy! Good puppy!" said Kat. She patted him and held him. She rewarded him with the dog treat.

They repeated the lesson three times. Each time, Houdini went to Kat when she asked.

"Okay. Time for more fun!" Kat decided. The girls spent the rest of the afternoon playing games with the puppy.

Finally, Grace glanced at her watch. "Time to go," she said. "I'm so excited that you two are coming over for dinner at my house!"

"Us too!" said Maya.

The girls took Houdini inside. They each gave him a quick kiss on the head before putting him in his crate. They picked up their backpacks. "See you tomorrow, Houdini," called Kat.

Tony and Marmalade were still in the reception area, but there was only one customer left.

"Tony, can I speak to Aunt Jenn for a minute?" asked Kat. "Is that okay?"

"Sure," said Tony. "Your aunt is just finishing her last groom of the day. Just poke your head in."

In a moment, Kat was back. "Aunt Jenn is going to call Mr. Ho and check with him about the party," she told Maya and Grace. "I told my aunt that I'm going to your house for dinner, Grace. I gave her your phone number. She said she'd call us there soon."

"Excellent!" said Maya

The girls waved goodbye to Tony and hurried out the door. They walked briskly toward Grace's house.

"Kat-nip, did you remember to bring the Puppy Collection?" asked Maya.

"Yup," said Kat. "It's in my backpack."

"Great! Let's work on it right after dinner," said Grace. "We can add Houdini to the collection."

Kat and Maya had come up with the idea for the Puppy Collection before the school year began. They couldn't have their own dogs, but they loved to collect photos of dogs and draw pictures of them. So they decided to collect them in a scrapbook. They gave each puppy a name and wrote about it. When they started helping at Tails Up, they began including the puppies that they met there. When Grace became their friend, they included her in the fun.

When they arrived at Grace's house, dinner was ready. The girls only had time to hang up their jackets and wash their hands.

"Please take a seat, one and all!" said Grace's dad. He waved a wooden spoon and wore a white apron splattered with tomato sauce. "I'll be right there!"

"Dad prepares dinner every Friday night,"

explained Grace, smiling. "It's always the same meal — his special meal."

"We suspect it's the only thing he *can* prepare," whispered Mrs. Ferguson. She winked at the girls.

"And for tonight, a special meal: spaghetti and meatballs with Caesar salad!" Mr. Ferguson announced. He carried in a tray with a big bowl of salad and a big plate of noodles covered in sauce and meatballs. Under his arm was a loaf of fresh bread.

"Wow!" sang out Grace. "What a yummy-looking surprise, Dad!"

Everyone helped themselves to pasta. Then Mrs. Ferguson went around the table sprinkling grated Parmesan cheese on everyone's noodles. Grace mixed the salad, clacking the serving spoons with a flourish. Maya showed off her noodle-twirling technique. Kat was cheerfully chasing meatballs around her plate with her fork.

When the delicious meal was over, the girls helped clear away the plates. Then Kat and Maya followed Grace upstairs.

Kat gasped when she entered Grace's bedroom. The walls were covered in posters and photos of dogs. The shelves of the bookcase were filled with books about dogs and even stuffed toy puppies.

"It's just like my room!" cried Kat.

"And like mine," added Maya.

Grace grinned. “Guess that’s because all three of us are—”

“Dog crazy!” cried all three girls at once.

Kat pulled the Puppy Collection scrapbook out of her backpack. Grace set out some coloured markers, pens, pencils, sticky tape and paper.

“Maya, how about you and I write a description of Houdini?” said Grace. “And Kat, will you draw some pictures of the puppy?”

“I’ll try,” Kat said. She didn’t think she was a

good artist, but she did love to draw puppies.

Kat sketched a picture of the beagle puppy running. She showed his long ears flying out behind him. She coloured him tan, black and white. She added a sparkle in his eyes. Then she drew a picture of him sneaking out of his crate, and another of him escaping out the back gate. Above these two drawings, she wrote *poof!*

"Okay. I think we're done," said Maya, after a while. "A masterpiece, as usual!"

Grace grinned and read it aloud. "*Houdini is a beagle puppy. He is three months old. He likes chasing balls and chasing sticks. He sits and lies down when we ask. But he is full of surprises! He is an escape artist, just like the real Houdini!*"

"I agree. It's a masterpiece," said Kat, grinning.

Just then, Grace's mom called up, "Katherine, your aunt is on the phone for you."

"I won't be able to come to the party tomorrow," Grace reminded the girls. "I'm spending the afternoon with my granny. But I sure hope Mr. Ho lets Houdini go to the party. It would be so much fun!"

Grace showed Kat to the phone, down the hallway. In a moment they were back with big grins on their faces.

"Mr. Ho says yes," Kat said. "Maya, you, Houdini and I are going to be guests at a dog birthday party tomorrow!"

CHAPTER SEVEN

"I'll pick you up in two hours, when the party is over," said Kat's mom. "Bye, Katherine! Bye, Maya. Take good care of that little puppy!" She gave a wave and drove off.

It was Saturday afternoon. Kat and Maya stood in the doorway of the Pet Party Palace. Kat held Houdini in her arms. Maya held a birthday gift for Charles's dog. It was a dog toy from Tails Up, donated by Aunt Jenn.

"A dog birthday party at a Pet Party Palace!" Kat laughed. She gave Houdini a kiss on his head. He wiggled excitedly.

"I've never been to a palace before. I'm so glad I dressed up!" Maya wore a tiara, a swooshy dress with sparkles and shiny shoes. She twirled with her arms wide, a magic wand in her hand.

Kat giggled. Being with Maya was never boring. Her friend liked to add pizzazz to almost every situation. She made everything more special.

"It's too bad Grace couldn't come today. She'd love this!" said Kat.

"We'll take lots of photos to show her," said Maya. "We can put them in the Puppy Collection."

Kat set Houdini down, and the puppy wagged his tail and immediately pulled toward the door.

"He knows where the fun is," said Maya. "Let's go in!"

As soon as they entered the Pet Party Palace, Kiera hurried over. "You're here! You're here!" The little girl crouched down beside the beagle puppy. "Hello, Houdini! Thank you so much for coming to be a party guest with me!"

Kiera took the girls over to meet her babysitter. "This is my babysitter, Sarah," Kiera told Kat and Maya. "And this is my cousin, Charles."

Charles smiled. "Hello," he said. "Thanks for coming to my dog's birthday party." There was a big St. Bernard sitting beside Charles. The St. Bernard had beautiful brown eyes surrounded by black markings. There was grey hair above his eyebrows and around his ears.

The boy put his hand on his dog's huge head. "This is Gustav. We call him Gus for short," said Charles. When he heard his name, the dog wagged his tail slowly. "Gus is an old guy, older than me even. I'm seven. He's ten today."

"Happy birthday, Gus," said Kat. She handed the

birthday gift to Charles and stroked Gus's head.

"And this is Houdini," said Kiera proudly. The beagle puppy was sitting very still. He looked tiny next to the giant St. Bernard.

"Say hello to Houdini, Gus," said Charles.

Gus lowered his head. He gently touched the puppy with his nose. Houdini's tail began to wag. He pushed at Gus's nose with his own nose.

Suddenly Gus's eyes lit up. Out came his tongue. He gave Houdini a huge, slobbery kiss, tipping Houdini off balance. The puppy scrambled back to his feet and, quick as a wink, gave Gus a kiss on his nose.

"A birthday kiss!" said Kiera, delighted.

Just then, a young man in a Pet Party Palace uniform made an announcement

"Welcome to all of Charles and Gus's party guests! This is the plan for this afternoon. We'll play two dog games. We'll have birthday cake.

Finally, we'll explore the amazing outdoor doggy maze. Now, please follow me to the party room!"

Kat and Maya looked at each other and tried not to giggle. Dog games? A birthday cake for a dog? A doggy maze?

Kat handed Houdini's leash to Kiera. "Why don't you walk Houdini to the party room?" she said.

Kiera's face lit up. "Okay!"

Sarah put her hand on the little girl's shoulder. "You'll remember the rules, Kiera, right? You can't go off on your own," Sarah said. "And you need to be responsible for this little puppy."

Kiera gave a solemn nod.

The walls of the party room were covered in colourful paw prints. Streamers and balloons dangled from the ceiling. There were picnic tables pushed up against the walls. Bowls of water for thirsty dog guests were placed on large plastic sheets on the floor. There were several

bins of dog treats and dog toys. Happy music was playing. Along the back wall was a closed door. Beside it was a sign: TO THE DOGGY MAZE.

"First," announced the party host, "let's all sing 'Happy Birthday' to Gus!"

As the children and the other guests sang, Gus sat calmly listening. Houdini stood alertly, his head turning here and there. Kat counted the other dog guests. There were two Labrador retrievers, Polly and Ash. There was a wheaten terrier named Bear and a boxer named Lincoln. There was Maxie, a German shepherd, and Target, who was a cockapoo, a cross between a poodle and a cocker spaniel. That meant there were eight dogs altogether.

"Now the first game is Follow My Command," said the party host. "Here's how we play. When I give a command, you ask your dog to follow it. The two dogs that obey last are out. We play until only two dogs are left. They will be the winners!"

"I'll take some photos of you and Houdini playing this game," Maya, holding up her camera, said to Kiera.

"Do you understand how to play?" Kat asked Kiera.

"I think so." Kiera nodded. "But can you help me?"

"Sure," said Kat. "By the way, I hope you don't expect Houdini to win this game. He's just a puppy and he only knows two commands!"

"That's okay," said Kiera cheerfully. "It's just for fun."

"I'll give you each some treats for your dogs," said the party host. "That will encourage them to do what you tell them!"

When he was finished handing out the treats, the party host asked everyone playing the game to stand in a line with their dogs. The wheaten terrier, Bear, barked excitedly. Lincoln, the boxer, jumped up on his owner over and over. Houdini wagged his tail. He kept turning his head here and there, looking at the other dogs.

"All ready?" asked the host. "Okay. The first command is *sit*."

Kat showed Kiera how to wait until she had Houdini's attention. She showed her to put the treat in one hand and lift the other hand slowly, palm down. "Sit, Houdini," said Kiera.

The beagle puppy hesitated for a moment, then he sat.

"Good puppy," Kiera cried. She offered Houdini the treat.

Bear, the wheaten, tried to play with Target and Ash. He would not listen to his owner. One of the Labs, Polly, lay down instead of sitting. Bear and Polly were out.

Now the host said, "The next command is *down*."

Kat showed Kiera the signal for *down*, which was holding her palm out, flat to the ground. She gave Kiera a treat to hold in her other hand.

"Down," said Kiera, making the hand signal. The beagle puppy hesitated, then he lay down.

"Good boy, Houdini!" cried Kiera. She gave him a treat and patted him.

Maya waved her wand at Kat and sent Houdini a thumbs-up.

The other Labrador retriever, Ash, and Target the cockapoo were out.

The next command was *roll over.*

"Sorry. Houdini doesn't know that command yet," Kat told Kiera.

"Oh well," said Kiera, shrugging. "That's okay." She remained crouched beside Houdini, patting him while the dogs did *roll over* and then *shake a paw.*

In the end, Gus and the boxer won.

"Hurray for Gus and Lincoln!" cried Kat. "And hurray for Houdini, who did very well for his age!"

CHAPTER EIGHT

"And now, a game of musical chairs," announced the party host.

"How can dogs play musical chairs?" Maya said to Kat. "This should be hilarious!"

The host put seven chairs in a large circle. "We'll play some music. The guests and their dogs must walk around the chairs. When the music stops, each guest must sit in a chair — and their dog must sit nicely in front of them.

The person and dog pair left without a chair when the music ends is out. We'll play until there is only one winning pair."

Kat scooped up Houdini and gave him a cuddle. "You are taking very good care of Kiera," she whispered to him. The beagle gave her nose a kiss.

"I know how to play musical chairs!" Kiera said excitedly. "Can I take Houdini on my own?"

"Okay," said Kat. "But remember, before you ask Houdini to sit, make sure he is looking right at you. Speak calmly to him. And whatever you do, don't let go of his leash. Don't let him do one of his escape acts!"

Kiera ran to join the others, holding tightly to Houdini's leash.

The music began. The eight pairs began to circle the chairs.

"Kat! Maya!" called Sarah, waving them over. She was standing with one of the Pet Party Palace staff.

"This is Paul, and he needs some help," Sarah explained when they joined her. "He needs to serve the birthday cake when this game ends. I said we'd help move the tables into place."

Kat and Maya were happy to lend a hand. They helped Paul move several tables. Then they helped put out the cups, plates, forks, napkins, placemats and even party hats. Everything was covered in doggy designs, such as colourful dog bones and different breeds of dogs.

About ten minutes later they were done. Maya had her wand in one hand and her camera in the other. "Let's hurry," she said. "I want to get some photos of Houdini playing this game, too."

But the musical chairs game was almost over. The music was still playing loudly, and there were two pairs left — Target and Polly and their owners — but only one chair.

"Too late," said Maya. "I guess Houdini and Kiera were bumped out."

Kat looked for the pair among the other children and dogs who were out of the game. She couldn't see them there.

Kat began to feel uneasy. She looked over at the other guests. Houdini and Kiera weren't there either.

Now Kat was scared. "Maya," Kat said, grabbing her friend's arm. "I can't find them. I don't see Houdini and Kiera anywhere!"

Maya was looking around frantically as well. "I don't see them either," she said, her voice shaking. "Where could they be, Kat? Where would Kiera go with Houdini?"

"I don't know," cried Kat.

"Or — wait," said Maya. "Do you think the puppy has done one of his disappearing acts again — and taken Kiera off somewhere with him?"

The girls stared at each other for a moment. Then Kat said, "Listen, Maya. Whatever has happened, we need to act fast. And first, we have to tell Sarah."

"Look. Sarah is over there." Maya pointed across the room. But as the girls began to hurry toward her, they saw Sarah stand on tiptoe and look all around the room. "I think she just realized they're gone," said Maya.

Sarah noticed that they were looking for Kiera, too. She signalled to them and mouthed "Where's Kiera?" Kat and Maya shook their heads to show her they didn't know. Then Sarah ran to the entrance at the front of the room. She spoke urgently to the staff member stationed there. Kat saw the woman shake her head, "no."

Suddenly Maya grabbed Kat's arm.

"Kat! Look!" Maya cried, pointing to the back wall of the party room. "The door. I just noticed. It was closed before. Now it's wide open."

"Oh no, Maya," said Kat. "Kiera and Houdini must have gone out there!"

CHAPTER NINE

"Let's go," cried Kat.

In a few moments, she and Maya were outside. They looked around frantically. They saw they were standing in a large paved area surrounded by a high chain-link fence. The only thing out there was a huge blue, red, yellow and green inflatable structure.

"The maze," said Maya breathlessly. "This must be the doggy maze."

"Yes," agreed Kat. "Oh, thank goodness this area is completely fenced in. They must be nearby still, in the maze, I guess."

"Do you think Kiera took Houdini in there?" asked Maya. "Why would she do that?"

"I don't know," said Kat, shaking her head. "I don't know why she wouldn't just wait until after the birthday cake . . ."

Suddenly Sarah appeared beside them. "I told the staff that Kiera's missing. They closed and locked the front door of the building straight away. And the main door of the party room, too," she said, speaking quickly. "But they're certain that Kiera and Houdini didn't go out that party room door. A staff person stays there during the whole party, just to make sure none of the children wander off. If they need to use the washroom, the staff member asks a parent or guardian to go with them."

"Okay," Maya said. "That's good, right?"

"Yes," Sarah agreed. She tried to catch her breath.

"If the only other way out of the party room is through this back door, then they must be out here," said Kat. "They *must* be in the maze."

"I agree," said Sarah. But she shook her head. "Kiera was so happy at the party with Houdini! I'm not sure why she would do this."

"Maybe Kiera let go of the leash for a moment and Houdini ran out here, and she came after him," said Kat, her voice wobbly. "We should have kept a closer eye on the puppy. We should have known he might do one of his escape acts!"

Sarah threw her arm over Kat's shoulders. "Don't worry. They must be together in the maze. A staff person is on her way to help find them."

"But we're not going to just stand here and wait, are we?" asked Maya, adjusting her tiara and waving her wand. "Let's go in and start the search! This princess is ready to rock and roll!"

"Yes, let's go," said Kat. "Kiera might be scared. Maybe she went in after Houdini and never found him! Maybe she's alone, and he's alone . . . ."

Woof! The dog bark came from right behind them.

Kat spun around. *Houdini?*

But no, it was Lincoln the boxer and his owner, a boy who looked about seven years old.

"I'm Sam," said the boy. "I just had to come out here and talk to you."

"What is it?" said Sarah, surprised.

The boy hung his head. "It's my fault that Kiera ran away."

"Your fault?" asked Kat, puzzled.

"I told her . . . I told her that she shouldn't really be at the party." Sam's voice quavered. "I told her that she doesn't have a dog and so she shouldn't be here."

Maya frowned. "Not cool," she said.

"I know," said Sam. "I only said it because she and Houdini were good at musical chairs and I . . . I wanted Lincoln and me to win. I'm sorry. I think I really hurt her feelings."

Lincoln woofed again, this time more loudly.

"Quiet, Lincoln," said Sam.

But Lincoln barked again and then again. The boxer was looking at the maze entrance. There was a happy little beagle and a little girl with a tear-stained face standing there!

CHAPTER TEN

"Kiera!" cried Sarah.

"Houdini!" cried Kat and Maya.

They hurried over. Sarah grabbed Kiera and hugged her, saying, "Oh, I'm so glad you're all right!"

Kat scooped up Houdini. It felt so good to hold him close. She breathed in his lovely puppy smell. She was so relieved that he was safe! She and Maya patted him over and over.

"Houdini," said Kat. "We were so scared!"

"You vanished on us again, you rascal," said Maya.

But Kiera cried, "No, no! Houdini isn't a rascal. He's wonderful! He didn't really run away." She took a deep breath. "I did. I ran away from the party because I was sad."

"Because of what I said," interrupted Sam. "I'm sorry, Kiera. That was mean, what I said to you."

Kiera shrugged. "Yes," she agreed. Then she shrugged again. "But what I did was bad, too. I dropped Houdini's leash, even though I knew I was responsible for him. I ran right out the back door, even though I told Sarah I wouldn't slip away. I shouldn't have done either of those things," Kiera said. "I'm sorry, Sarah, and Kat and Maya. I'm sorry, Houdini," she added, petting the puppy. "But thanks for running after me."

Houdini wagged his tail.

"I ran into the maze, and I turned this way and that way, and then I was completely lost. I couldn't find my way back out again!" Kiera said.

"You must have been scared," said Sam, sympathetically.

"No," said Kiera, indignantly. "I wasn't scared." She crossed her arms. "I was angry. I realized running away was wrong and dumb. I couldn't find my way back, and I didn't want to miss having a piece of birthday cake!"

Kat and Maya smiled at each other.

"But it was okay, because Houdini came after me and he found me, didn't you, puppy?"

Houdini wagged his tail "yes."

"Suddenly there he was! *Presto!* Like magic!" Kiera cried. "And he led me right out of the maze!"

"You're a hero, Houdini!" Kat whispered to the puppy. Houdini wagged his tail even harder.

"Okay, so let's go back in," suggested Sam. "We might be just in time for the cake! I checked it out. There's one cake for people and one cake for dogs."

"I bet you'd like some cake. Right, Houdini?" Kiera asked the puppy.

Houdini struggled in Kat's arms.

Kat and Maya exchanged a look. Kiera had not been responsible with Houdini, but she had apologized.

"Vanishing isn't the only kind of magic you do, is it, Houdini?" Kat whispered to the puppy. She set Houdini down and handed Kiera the leash. "Here you go, Kiera," she said. "Just remember . . ."

"I know," Kiera said, grinning. "I'll take really good care of him. And this time, I won't let go of him for anything. I promise!"

They all hurried back into the party room just in time to sing "Happy Birthday" to Charles's dog, Gus. And Sam was right. There was a regular cake with purple frosting for people. There was a cake for dogs as well. It had a top layer of liver. The bottom layer was peanut butter and banana. On each cake was written, *Happy Birthday, Gus!*

Everyone got a slice. The people sat at the picnic tables with their cake. The dogs ate their pieces from plastic plates set on the floor. Kiera took a little puppy-sized piece of cake for Houdini, and she stood near him holding his leash while he gobbled up his cake.

She even managed to put a party hat on the puppy. Houdini wasn't sure if he liked it or not. He cocked his head. He wrinkled his nose.

But then Lincoln grabbed Houdini's party hat in his teeth, pulled it off and chewed it to pieces. Houdini didn't seem to mind.

"And now, the amazing maze!" announced the party host. "Everyone, please bring your dogs this way!"

"Do you promise to hold Houdini's leash the whole time?" Kat asked Kiera.

"I promise," said Kiera. "I won't let him vanish — and I won't vanish either."

Houdini wagged his tail.

"But it won't be fair," said Maya, with a smile. "You and Houdini have already had a sneak preview!"

Kiera grinned. Houdini's eyes sparkled.

"Okay. Off you go, you two," said Kat.

Kiera raced after Sam with Houdini bounding along beside her on his leash.

CHAPTER ELEVEN

"Houdini! How was the birthday party?" Grace scooped up the beagle puppy and peered into his sparkling brown eyes. Out came Houdini's tongue. He gave Grace's nose a quick kiss.

The three girls were at Tails Up. They had come to say goodbye to Houdini before Mr. Ho arrived to take him home.

"It was lots of fun," said Maya. "Houdini and Kiera loved it! But . . ."

Maya and Kat shared a look.

"Uh-oh," said Grace. She made a fierce face at Houdini. "Were you naughty again, you little escape artist?"

"Actually," Kat said, "Houdini was a hero!" She explained to Grace how Kiera had hidden in the maze and gotten lost, and how Houdini had helped the girl find her way out.

"Oh, what a good boy!" cooed Grace. She set the puppy down. "And now, let's have some fun!"

Grace threw a dog toy across the room. Houdini raced after it and then pounced. As he shook the toy, his ears flew from side to side.

"Houdini, you are so cute!" giggled Maya.

"I wish we had more time with Houdini," Kat said . "Mr. Ho will be back this afternoon!"

"Cheer up, Kat-nip! We still have all morning." Maya pulled out her camera. "And we can take more photos of Houdini and put them in our Puppy Collection!"

"That's true," said Kat. She grinned. The day wasn't over yet! There was still lots of fun ahead with her two friends and the sweet puppy, Houdini.

Houdini
Houdini is a beagle puppy. He
is three months old. He likes
chasing balls and sticks. He
sits and lies down when we
ask. But he is full of
surprises! He is an escape
artist just like the real
Houdini!

POOF!
Houdini
Kat
STAMP
BLUE

For more Puppy Collection fun, check out these other books in the series.

ISBN 978-1-4431-2409-6

ISBN 978-1-4431-2410-2

ISBN 978-1-4431-2411-9

ISBN 978-1-4431-3358-6

ISBN 978-1-4431-3360-9

ISBN 978-1-4431-3362-3